Oddies, Maritime House, Grafton Square, London, SW4 0JW

Text copyright © Oddies 2008
Illustrations copyright © Oddies 2008

A CIP catalogue record for this book is available from the British Library.

First published in Great Britain in 2004 by Oddies Limited.

ISBN-10:   1-904745-12-1
ISBN-13:   978-1-904745-12-9

Printed in China

Police
Oddie

Grant Slatter

The policeman put his favourite pair of socks into the washing machine. He added some washing powder and shut the door.

"Chug-chug, whirr, chug-chug, whirr," went the washing machine. Then it did something strange.

It spun extra fast and all the bubbles bounced around wildly. The machine ballooned. Then there was a supersonic WHOOSH as one of the socks disappeared.

The sock was called Police Oddie and he was zooming through space towards Oddieworld. "I hope everyone is being good," he said.

Police Oddie floated down into Oddieworld and popped out of his bubble.
"Can you help me?" said a soft voice behind him.

It was Sock Fairy. "Someone's been muddling up all the signs - look," she said. Police Oddie looked round but when he turned back, Sock Fairy had disappeared.

She had left a shiny new whistle in her place as a gift. "That's useful," said Police Oddie, "I can whistle for help if I need to."

Then Police Oddie heard some banging. Builder Oddie was repairing a sign. "All the signs between here and Darn Farm have been messed up," he said.

"Hmmm," said Police Oddie. "I think I'd better follow the muddled signs until I catch up with the culprit."
"Ok, I'll follow on behind you fixing," said Builder Oddie.

There was a big bang and a puff of smoke.

When the smoke cleared, Police Oddie started to laugh. Wizzo's spell had gone wrong, as usual.

"Perhaps this will shed some light on the problem," bubbled Police Oddie.

He didn't notice that the spell had also made the little ball inside his whistle disappear.

Police Oddie went round the edge of Wiggly Woods and passed Fairy Cottage. There was another muddled sign.

He hurried on to Darn Farm. He was sure that whoever was doing this was not far away.

As soon as he arrived he spotted some Oddies by the stable.
It was Robber Oddie, Pirate Oddie and Scribbler Oddie.
"I knew it!" said Police Oddie. "Bad Oddies!"

"I'll blow my whistle to call for help!" said Police Oddie. He blew it very hard but it made no sound. "Oh no," he cried, "what's happened to my whistle?"

He blew it again. It still didn't make any sound, but a pack of dogs came running around the corner, barking loudly.

The Bad Oddies were so scared that they turned themselves inside out - into little sock balls.

Police Oddie laughed. "Wizzo's crazy spell must have turned my whistle into a 'silent' whistle - only dogs can hear it now!"

Builder Oddie heard the barking and hurried over. "You caught them!" he said. "At last I can stop mending signs."

"I hope you'll put them in jail," he added.
"No, I've got a better idea," smiled Police Oddie.

"You know best," said Builder Oddie. "Well done anyway."
"Yes well done," said a familiar voice.

It was Sock Fairy. "We'd love you to stay in Oddieworld forever," she said, "but I'll magic you back if that's what you'd really like."

"Well, with all these Bad Oddies causing trouble, I think I better stay," replied Police Oddie. "It seems Oddieworld could do with my help!"

That night Builder Oddie had a party to celebrate, but some Oddies were busy elsewhere...

Pirate Oddie, Robber Oddie and Scribbler Oddie had to scrub the jail clean!

Back home, the policeman searched until bedtime for his missing sock but he couldn't find it anywhere.

As he lay in bed he asked himself...

"Where do those odd socks go?"

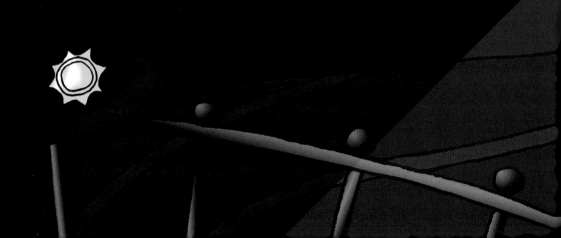

Do you have the complete collection?

The Story of Oddieworld
Grant Slatter

Police Oddie
Grant Slatter

Horse Rider Oddie
Grant Slatter

Footy Oddie
Grant Slatter

Nurse Oddie
Grant Slatter

Robber Oddie
Grant Slatter

Ballet Oddie
Grant Slatter

Pirate Oddie
Grant Slatter

Princess Oddie
Grant Slatter

Santa Oddie

Angel Oddie
Grant Slatter

MAIN SERIES

Super Hero Oddie
Edited by Grant Slatter

Brownie Oddie

Cub Scout Oddie
Tomasz Nicholls Matthew Tither Grant Slatter

Wrestler Oddie
Sam Taylor Danny Bird Grant Slatter

Rainbow Oddie
Gina Bird Grant Slatter

Beaver Scout Oddie
Christopher Crowe Grant Slatter

SPECIAL SERIES

Adapted from Oddies stories written by children.

Step into your favourite character!

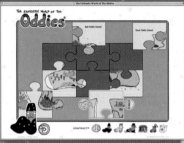

Take a trip to...

Oddieworld!

WWW.ODDIEWORLD.COM

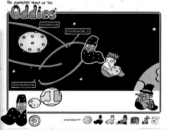

EXPLORE

Play FREE games and
find the secret game area.

DISCOVER

How do Oddies pick things up?
How do they move? The
answers are revealed.

JOIN

Become an Oddies Friend
and we'll send you a FREE
Oddies book and poster!

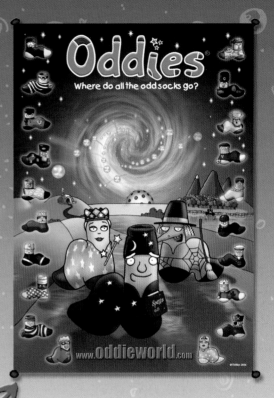

www.oddieworld.com

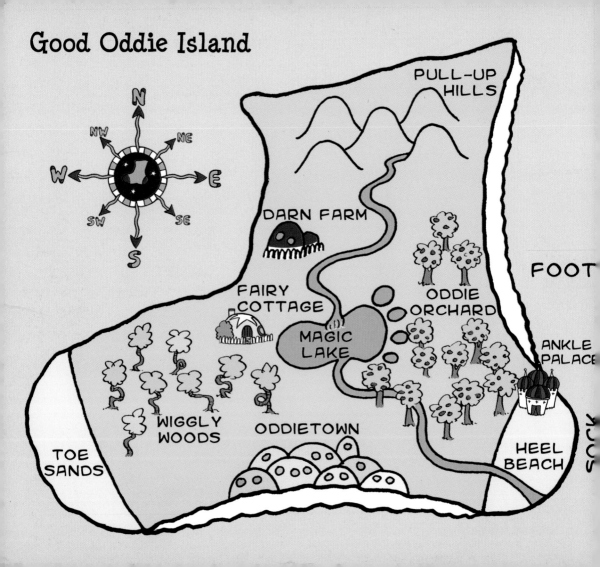